# Penguin's Special Christmas Tree

written by

## Jeannie St. John Taylor

## illustrated by Molly Idle

Published by Lobster Press™
1620 Sherbrooke Street West, Suites C & D
Montréal, Québec   H3H 1C9
Tel. (514) 904-1100 • Fax (514) 904-1101
www.lobsterpress.com

Publisher: Alison Fripp
Editors: Alison Fripp & Meghan Nolan
Editorial Assistant: Faye Smailes
Graphic Design & Production: Tammy Desnoyers

*Société de développement des entreprises culturelles*
Québec

We acknowledge the support of the government of Québec, tax credit for book publishing, administered by SODEC.

Library and Archives Canada Cataloguing in Publication

St. John Taylor, Jeannie, 1945-
    Penguin's special Christmas tree / Jeannie St. John Taylor ; Molly Idle, illustrator.

ISBN 978-1-897073-61-2 (bound)
ISBN 978-1-897073-64-3 (pbk.)

    1. Penguins--Juvenile fiction.  2. Christmas stories, American.  I. Idle, Molly Schaar  II. Title.

PZ7.T357Pe 2007            j813'.6            C2007-901251-5

Printed and bound in Singapore.

To Ty, Tori, Tevin, and Kirsten

— *Jeannie St. John Taylor*

For Evan and Randy

— *Molly Idle*

"I want to **win** 'Santa's Best Tree' award this year, but I can't find anything for the **top** of the tree."

# Got it!"

"Too much *green*?"

"Let's try
working together."

"Santa *loves* handmade stuff."

"Not enough color?"

"This just won't work.
Let's try a smaller snowman."

"*This* size is better."

"I'll get the mop."

"Nobody else will have something like this on the top!"

"Wait!"

"I know!
Let's put Harold on top!"

"Great idea!"

"Harold *monkeys* around too much."

"Maybe we need something
that **lights up!**"

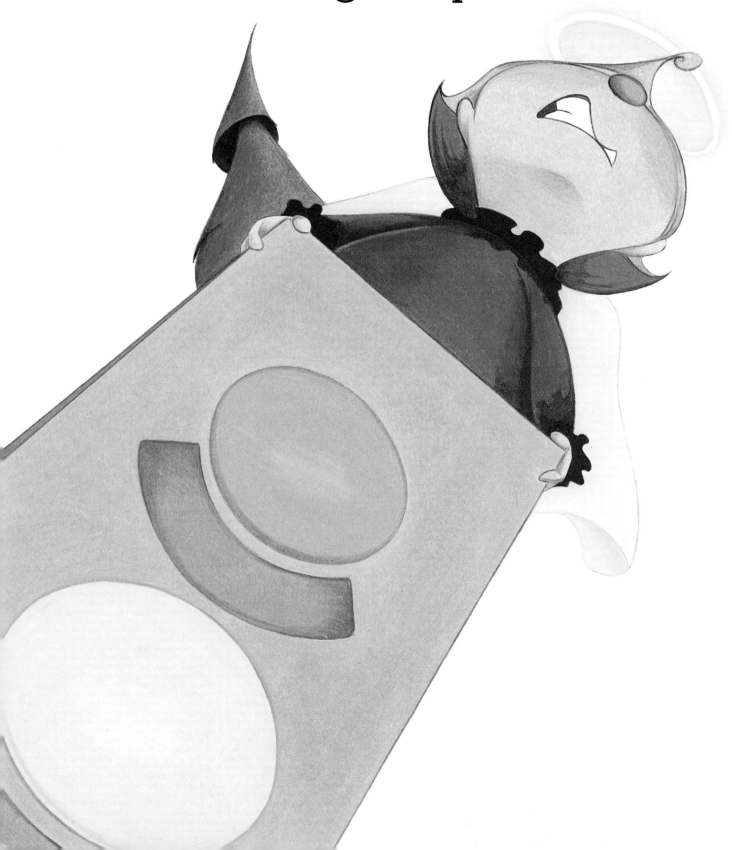

"Wait until you see **this**!"

"Are you out of ideas now?"

"Yes."

"Me too. I'll never finish in time. I'm so sad! I *really* want to **win** the **award**! What will I do?"

"I wish I knew how
to help."

"Hey! Wait. GREAT idea.
Stay there. Don't move.
Up a little higher.
Move that way.
A little more ... more.
Too much. Go back.

Perfect!"

"You won!
Santa loves your tree!"

"We won.
I couldn't have done it without you."